Dear Parent:

This story is rich with opportunities for us to understand some of what goes on in the minds of young children.

We begin with Clifford's good intention to stay clean (because his loving owner, Emily Elizabeth, has asked him to). He gives up doing many of his favorite things, since they might get him dirty. Not surprisingly, though, his resolve is not strong enough to resist a temptation that comes his way. Clifford has the limited self-control typical of a young child. He, too, readily succumbs to the beckoning of pleasure. Reading about Clifford's lost resolve offers parents a wonderful opportunity to hear, indirectly, about what goes on inside the minds of their children who feel compelled to do something forbidden or unwise.

As the story progresses, Clifford tries to undo his mistake by heading for a cleansing car wash. Hearing that, children will be rooting for him—for they, too, hope to follow their wishes while somehow avoiding parental rebuke. Then, all at once, the situation changes. There is an emergency, and the cleanliness issue fades. Things get even better, from a child's point of view, when Clifford goes to the rescue and turns out to be a hero.

Haven't grown-ups said that it's important to help others when they're in need? Well, Clifford does it, and his Emily is so proud. Children will enjoy the triumph with him when Clifford lives out their shared heroic fantasy. Pretending to be rescuers allows little ones to feel strong and competent, rather than small and dependent on the approval of grown-ups.

Adele M. Brodkin, Ph.D.

Visit Clifford at scholastic.com/clifford

ISBN 0-439-24069-7

Library of Congress Cataloging-in-Publication Data

10 9 8 7 6 5 4 3 2 1   01 02 03 04 05 06

Printed in the U.S.A.
First printing, August 2001

Clifford THE BIG RED DOG®
The Big Red Mess

Adapted by Bob Barkly

Illustrated by Jim Durk

**Based on the Scholastic book series
"Clifford The Big Red Dog"
by Norman Bridwell**

From the television script
"A Ferry Tale"

SCHOLASTIC INC.

New York   Toronto   London   Auckland   Sydney   Mexico City
New Delhi   Hong Kong

Rub-a-dub-dub,
Clifford got a good scrub
From the tip of his nose
To the nails on his toes.

"Clifford," said Emily,
"Don't you look clean!
You're the handsomest dog
That I've ever seen.
You should be on the cover
Of *Prize Pooch* magazine!

Today they are choosing

The Dog of the Year.

I can definitely picture

My big red dog here.

Judge Lily LaValley

Is coming here soon.

She'll be on the island

This afternoon."

Then Emily told Clifford

Not to get dirty,

And to be on the dock

At exactly four-thirty.

She gave him a hug

And a kiss on the snout.

"Bye-bye! See you later,"

She said, and went out.

Now, Clifford knew Emily

Didn't *mean* to be mean,

But that was asking a lot—

For him to stay clean.

Clean meant N-O to digging,

To swimming and rolling...

A dog could get dirty

While running or strolling.

So Clifford just lay there
And lay there some more.
Till he suddenly heard
Two loud barks out the door....

It was T-Bone and Cleo.
They wanted to play.
"I'd love to," said Clifford,
"But just not today.
I have to stay clean—
At least till four-thirty—
The Dog of the Year's
Not supposed to be dirty."

"Oh, please, Clifford, please,"
Cleo started to moan.
"We just came from the pier,
Where we smelled a great bone.
It smelled juicy and meaty,
And perfectly grand."
"But it's buried," groaned T-Bone,
"Way down in the sand."

Well, that's all
Clifford had to hear.
"Come on," he called.
"I'll race you there!"
And off he galloped
To the pier.

Clifford dug with his heart,

And he dug with his soul.

He dug and he dug

A really huge hole!

And way down in the bottom,

Way down in the muck,

He found his great treasure...

"Oh, no! Look at me!"
Clifford let out a wail.
He was filthy and wet
From his ears to his tail.

"But wait!" said Clifford.
"I know a place
Where I can wash
My paws and face.
There's a car wash
At the edge of town.
Just follow me—
They'll hose me down."

Rub-a-dub-dub,

Clifford got a good scrub

From the tips of his toes...

Halfway up to his nose!

The rest of his bath

Would have to wait.

He looked at the clock:

It was getting late.

Lickety-split—

Clifford raced to the pier.

But Judge Lily LaValley

Still wasn't near.

She was stuck on the ferry,

A mile out or two,

Surrounded by fog

Too thick to sail through.

It seemed hard to believe,

But it really was true:

There was nothing, no nothing,

The captain could do.

But suddenly Clifford

Dove in from the shore.

He swam and he swam

And he swam out some more.

He looped the towrope

Beneath his chin,

And he swam and he swam

And he towed the boat in.

Dockside stood Emily,
Beaming with pride.
"Hooray for Clifford!"
Judge Lily cried.
"This big brave red dog
Brought me in from the fog.
So let's all give a cheer...

For the Dog of the Year!"

BOOKS IN THIS SERIES:

Welcome to Birdwell Island: Everyone on Birdwell Island thinks that Clifford is just too big! But when there's an emergency, Clifford The Big Red Dog teaches everyone to have respect—even for those who are different.

A Puppy to Love: Emily Elizabeth's birthday wish comes true: She gets a puppy to love! And with her love and kindness, Clifford The Small Red Puppy becomes Clifford The Big Red Dog!

The Big Sleep Over: Clifford has to spend his first night without Emily Elizabeth. When he has trouble falling asleep, his Birdwell Island friends work together to make sure that he—and everyone else—gets a good night's sleep.

No Dogs Allowed: No dogs in Birdwell Island Park? That's what Mr. Bleakman says—before he realizes that sharing the park with dogs is much more fun.

An Itchy Day: Clifford has an itchy patch! He's afraid to go to the vet, so he tries to hide his scratching from Emily Elizabeth. But Clifford soon realizes that it's better to be truthful and trust the person he loves most—Emily Elizabeth.

The Doggy Detectives: Oh, no! Emily Elizabeth is accused of stealing Jetta's gold medal—and then her shiny mirror! But her dear Clifford never doubts her innocence and, with his fellow doggy detectives, finds the real thief.

Follow the Leader: While playing follow-the-leader with Clifford and T-Bone, Cleo learns that playing fair is the best way to play!

The Big Red Mess: Clifford tries to stay clean for the Dog of the Year contest, but he ends up becoming a big red mess! However, when Clifford helps the judge reach the shore safely, he finds that he doesn't need to stay clean to be the Dog of the Year.

The Big Surprise: Poor Clifford. It's his birthday, but none of his friends will play with him. Maybe it's because they're all busy. . . planning his surprise party!

The Wild Ice Cream Machine: Charley and Emily Elizabeth decide to work the ice cream machine themselves. Things go smoothly. . . until the lever gets stuck and they find themselves knee-deep in ice cream!

Dogs and Cats: Can dogs and cats be friends? Clifford, T-Bone, and Cleo don't think so. But they have a change of heart after they help two lost kittens find their mother.

The Magic Ball: Emily Elizabeth trusts Clifford to deliver a package to the post office, but he opens it and breaks the gift inside. Clifford tries to hide his blunder, but Emily Elizabeth appreciates honesty and understands that accidents happen.